UNASSIGNED LANDS

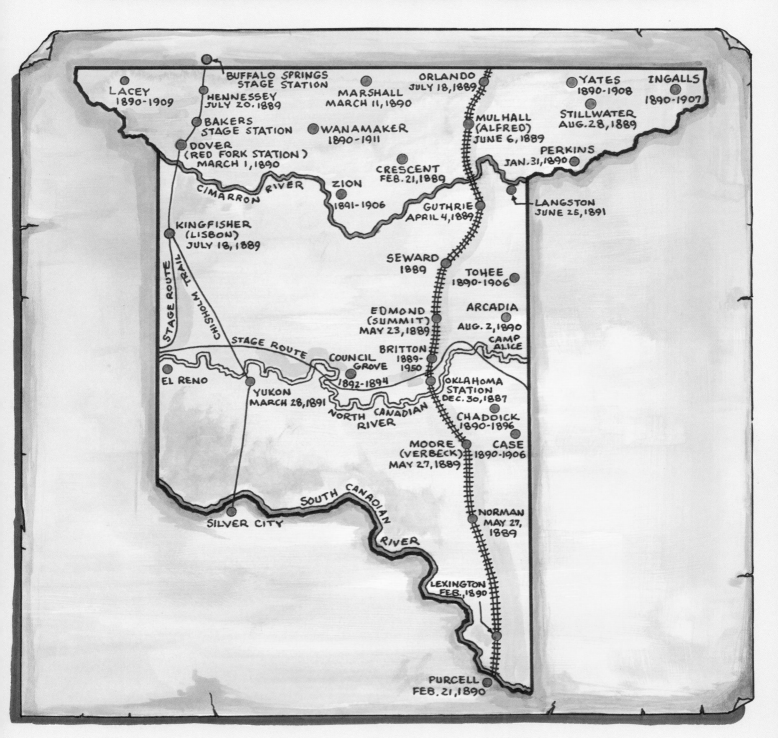

The Oklahoma LAND RUN

To Dixie

The Oklahoma LAND RUN

By Una Belle Townsend
Illustrated by Emile Henriquez

Una Belle Townsend

PELICAN PUBLISHING COMPANY
GRETNA 2009

To V.P.—the "Okie" who introduced me to Oklahoma

The word "Pelican" and the depiction of a pelican are trademarks of Pelican Publishing Company, Inc., and are registered in the U.S. Patent and Trademark Office.

Library of Congress Cataloging-in-Publication Data

Townsend, Una Belle.
  The Oklahoma Land Run / by Una Belle Townsend ; illustrated by Emile Henriquez.
      p. cm.
  Summary: Nine-year-old Jesse convinces his injured father to let him drive the wagon during the 1889 Oklahoma Land Rush.
  ISBN 978-1-58980-566-8 (hardcover : alk. paper) 1. Oklahoma—History—Land Rush, 1889—Juvenile fiction. [1. Oklahoma—History—Land Rush, 1889—Fiction 2. Fathers and sons—Fiction. 3. Responsibility—Fiction.] I. Henriquez, Emile F., ill. II. Title.
  PZ7.T6665Ok 2009
  [E]—dc22

                                    2008030448

Printed in Singapore

Published by Pelican Publishing Company, Inc.
1000 Burmaster Street, Gretna, Louisiana 70053

THE OKLAHOMA LAND RUN

"I can do it, Pa. I know I can," said Jesse, as he fed the horses, Ben and Bob, in the shed.

"Son, you're too young and it's dangerous," answered Pa. "Hundreds of people will be there—maybe thousands. Our horses are strong, but if they get excited, they'll be hard to handle."

Pa tried to get his shoulder and arm in a better position in his sling. His fall last week had been a bad one.

Tomorrow would be April 22, 1889. At noon, two million acres called the "Unassigned Lands" would be given to settlers in a land run. Now, his dream of pounding a stake in the ground to claim 160 acres of free land in the Oklahoma Territory would not come true. Tugging at his sling again, he knew he couldn't even drive his wagon!

"Pa," Jesse pleaded. "It's our only chance. You've let me drive before."

"You're right, Jesse. I guess you'll have to drive the team tomorrow," Pa said, picking up a wooden stake with his good hand. "I'll be there beside you, but I just don't like the idea of my nine-year-old son racing against grown men." He threw the stake to the ground.

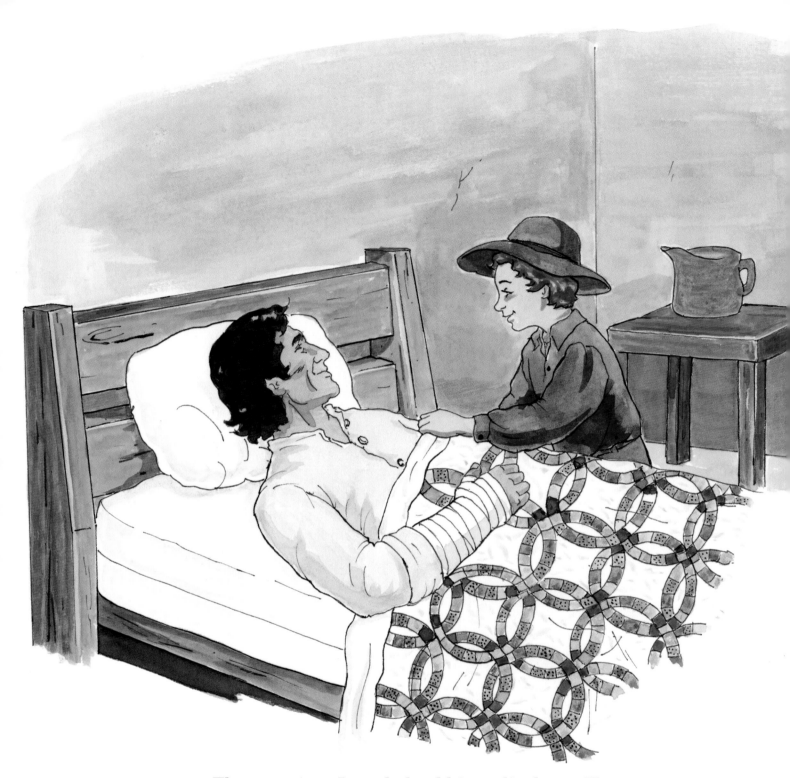

That evening, Jesse helped his pa lie down. He pulled a quilt over him and said, "Pa, I can do it. I'll get us some land."

When it was time to go to the starting line the next morning, Ma gave them a dinner bucket with beans, biscuits, and jerky in it. Jesse helped Pa climb into the wagon.

"Get close to the front," said Pa. "We'll have to look out for 'sooners.' They'll have their claim registered before most of us can put a stake in the ground."

At the starting line, they waited for the signal to begin. Men pushed past them on horseback. Others in wagons and in one-horse buggies wiggled their way toward the starting line. A few on bicycles and on foot tried to sneak ahead of the others.

"Whoa! Get back behind the line," shouted a tall soldier on horseback as he patrolled the starting area. The men turned around and joined the others. One family tried to hide in a clump of bushes. "Move back," yelled the tall Fort Reno cavalryman.

"Pa, a captain over there says the trains are full of people ready to jump off for some of the free land," said Jesse. "You reckon that's true?"

"Don't know," said Pa. "There must be a hundred wagons around here. I'm sure there are plenty of people on trains, too."

The impatient crowd continued to push toward the starting line. As it neared noon, the settlers became quiet.

At twelve o'clock, a cannon's blast shattered
the silence. Riders on horses darted out in front.

"Yee-haw!" yelled Jesse, slapping the reins to his horses. Ben and Bob sprang forward.

The rumblings of horses' hooves and wagon wheels filled the air. Dust flew everywhere. Jesse's eyes stung. He and Pa gasped for some fresh air.

Jesse's heart pounded wildly. He had a tight grasp on the reins. Within a few minutes, his hands throbbed. He relaxed his grip a little. It would be a long race.

A rough-looking man in a nearby wagon yelled, "Get outta my way, boy! Young'ns your age shouldn't be a-drivin'." He grabbed his whip and boomed at his horses, "Faster, I said, faster!"

He tried squeezing his wagon between Jesse's and another one. For a moment, Jesse thought their wheels would lock together, tearing up Pa's wagon!

Tightening his grip on the reins again, Jesse yelled, "What'll I do, Pa?"

"Hold her steady and keep her straight," said Pa. "You'll be all right."

The burly man charged to the front, scattering dirt over all the wagons he passed. Jesse and his Pa breathed in the swirling dust and coughed.

"Pa, my eyes feel gritty!" shouted Jesse. He wiped his face and blew dirt from his lips.

"Keep driving, son," said Pa. He winced in pain as the wagon bumped along the uneven prairie.

Before long, they noticed a few people slowing down. Some were working on broken wagon wheels. Others took care of lame horses.

"Pa, there's a pond over there with some cedar trees around it. Let's claim that land," said Jesse as he slowed the horses.

As they got closer, they saw a red-haired man standing under a tree. His horse gulped water at the pond. "Move on," he yelled, holding up his hammer and stake. "This land's mine!"

Pa sighed, shifted in his seat, and said, "Jesse, turn the horses toward that little hill over there."

Jesse looked around him as the horses climbed to the top of the hill. He said, "I like this land, Pa. There's a creek in the valley and wild-flowers growing on the hillside. There's even some mistletoe hanging in the trees."

"I like it, too," said Pa. "We could build a house
over by those trees and plant a big garden."

"Whoa, Ben. Whoa, Bob," said Jesse, pulling the wagon up to the creek. The thirsty horses stretched their necks toward the water.

"I'll look for the surveyor's stone," said Jesse as he jumped from the wagon. He knew Pa needed the information on it to claim the land. Jesse ran up and down the hill and then toward the creek, searching for the stone. "I've got to find it," he thought.

After a few minutes, he yelled, "Look, Pa! I think that's the stone we're looking for—the one near the top of the hill on the other side of the creek."

He grabbed the hammer and stake and ran toward the water. Taking a deep breath, he splashed through the creek. It was cold, but he didn't care.

He raced up the hill and saw the surveyor's stone near a pile of rocks. He quickly placed Pa's stake next to it.

Then he pounded the stake in the hard ground until it was deep in the dirt. Turning toward his pa, he threw his hat in the air. "We did it, Pa!" he yelled. "We did it!"

He knew the next few years would be busy
ones. They would have to build a house and
improve the land in order to keep it.

Right now, though, he couldn't wait to tell his
ma about the wildflowers in bloom. She'd like
that. What he'd like, though, was fishing and
swimming in the creek.

By proclamation of President Benjamin Harrison, designated areas as outlined, are to be open for settlement at and after the hour of twelve o'clock, noon, on the twenty second day of April next, and not before.